Hello, Moon

JULIE DOWNING

NEAL PORTER BOOKS
HOLIDAY HOUSE / NEW YORK

Hello, moon.

Goodbye, sun.

Night is near.

Day is done.

Look above,
silver skies.

Stir awake,
open eyes.

Moonlight calls,
come outside.

pounce

scurry

glide

flutter

Listen now.

peep

chatter

and hoot

and chirp

bark

and squeak

Ripe, red fruit,
savory seeds.

Midnight feast,
tender leaves.

Beware above.
Run and hide!
Silent swoop.

Safe inside.

Cloudy moon,
rustling leaves.

Branches bow,
cool night breeze.

Wild winds blow,
lightning flash.

Thunder roars!
Raindrops splash.

Hurry home.
Almost there.

Warm and dry,
cozy lair.

Come in close,
curl up tight.
Close your eyes,
almost light.

Sweet dreams, stars.
Good morning, bright.

Hello, day!

Goodbye, night!

To Lyla, Josie, and Parker

Neal Porter Books

Text and illustrations copyright © 2121 by Julie Downing
All Rights Reserved
HOLIDAY HOUSE is registered in the U.S. Patent and Trademark Office.
Printed and bound in January 2021 at C & C Offset, Shenzhen, China.
The artwork for this book was created with colored pencil, watercolor, and liquid acrylics
on cold press watercolor paper. The paintings were combined digitally.
www.holidayhouse.com
First Edition
1 3 5 7 9 10 8 6 4 2

Library of Congress Cataloging-in-Publication Data

Names: Downing, Julie, author, illustrator.
Title: Hello Moon / by Julie Downing.
Description: First edition. | New York : Holiday House, [2021] | "A Neal
Porter Book." | Audience: Ages 4 to 8. | Audience: Grades K–1. |
Summary: Illustrations and easy-to-read, rhyming text reveal the
nighttime activities of forest animals that awake when the Sun sets and the Moon rises.
Identifiers: LCCN 2020025784 | ISBN 9780823447015 (hardcover)
Subjects: CYAC: Stories in rhyme. | Nocturnal animals—Fiction. | Forest
animals—Fiction. | Night—Fiction. | Bedtime—Fiction.
Classification: LCC PZ8.3.D75398 Hel 2021 | DDC [E]—dc23
LC record available at https://lccn.loc.gov/2020025784

ISBN 978-0-8234-4701-5 (hardcover)